THE GREAT CAR RALLY

Rosie Heywood

Designed and illustrated by
Brenda Haw

Edited by Philippa Wingate
Managing designer: Mary Cartwright

Contents

Cover design: Jan McCafferty

Entering the rally

Aunt Lucy has entered the Great Car Rally, and she's asked her nephew Dan to help her. He's been learning how to read maps, so that he can tell Aunt Lucy which way to go during the rally.

Aunt Lucy has given Dan a copy of the rally rules.

Rally rules
*Any type of car can enter the Great Car Rally.
*Seat belts must be fastened before starting.
*Cars must start one after the other.
*Each car will be carefully timed.
*The car to reach the finish line with the fastest time is the winner.
*The winners will have their names put on the Great Car Rally cup.
*Watch out for red and yellow striped flags, they mean "Danger up ahead!".

This year, the Great Car Rally is going to be filmed, so that it can be shown on television. On each double page, look for a member of the film crew with a television camera.

There are puzzles to solve on every page. See if you can solve them all and help Aunt Lucy and Dan win the Great Car Rally. If you get stuck, the answers are on pages 31 and 32.

About the car

This is Aunt Lucy's race car. She's put a new turbo-booster into the engine, which she hopes will make it go much faster.

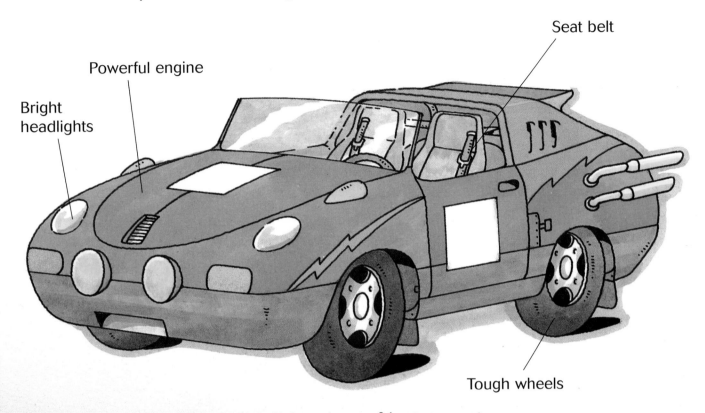

Seat belt

Powerful engine

Bright
headlights

Tough wheels

This is the car's dashboard. It has lots of instruments that help Aunt Lucy to drive.

Fuel gauge – shows
her how much fuel
is left.

Speedometer – tells
her how fast the car
is going.

Red light –
flashes when
the fuel level
is low.

Yellow light –
flashes when
the oil level is
low.

Blue light – comes
on when the brake
fluid level is low.

Here are Aunt Lucy's top driving tips:
1. Use first gear to go up steep hills.
2. Always put the handbrake on when you stop.

At the starting line

The day of the Great Car Rally is sunny and bright. Aunt Lucy and Dan drive to the starting point and line up behind the other cars.

"Look at all these fantastic cars," says Dan. "Do you know any of the drivers?"

"Well I know the Fume Brothers. Their car is yellow with red splotches," replies Aunt Lucy. "Wilma Wheelspin's car is blue with yellow spots, and Angus Automatic's is green with only three wheels.

Dan soon spotted everybody. Can you?

4

Fifteen minutes later, Aunt Lucy and Dan reach the front of the line. It's their turn to start! As soon as the starter lowers his flag, Aunt Lucy and Dan zoom forward. Dan quickly notes down the time.

At what time did Dan and Aunt Lucy start the rally?

Which way?

Before long, Dan and Aunt Lucy arrive at a junction with five roads all leading off in different directions.

"Which way should we go?" asks Aunt Lucy.

"We need to head toward Axle Mountain," replies Dan, looking at his map. Then he reads the big board beside the road, and looks carefully at the signposts at the beginning of each road. He soon knows which one to take.

Do you know which road leads to Axle Mountain?

Pedal Hill

Wheelie Valley

Axle Mountain

Brake Lake

Mirror Wood

As they speed off down the road to Axle Mountain, Aunt Lucy looks at the dashboard. A yellow light is flashing on and off.

Can you remember what a yellow flashing light means?

Trouble ahead

"The yellow flashing light means the engine needs more oil," says Aunt Lucy. "We'll have to stop."

While Aunt Lucy pours some oil into the engine, Dan gets out of the car and looks around. Up ahead, he can see a mountain goat walking across the road. Dan knows he will have to look out for other dangers along the way.

Can you spot five other dangers?

Soon they are ready to set off again. Dan guides Aunt Lucy past the dangers. As they reach the top of Axle Mountain, the road becomes steeper and steeper. Aunt Lucy quickly changes gears.

Do you know which gear she has changed to?

Forest trails

On the other side of Axle Mountain, Dan and Aunt Lucy enter a dark forest. Ahead of them, they can see lots of muddy trails, twisting and turning through the trees.

Dan knows he must find a way through the forest, and make sure they don't waste any time by driving down dead ends.

Can you see which is the quickest route out of the forest?

"Well done Dan," says Aunt Lucy. "My watch says it's eleven-thirty. How long have we been traveling?"

Dan checks their start time in his notebook and calculates the answer.

Do you know how long they have been traveling?

Puncture problem

As they leave the forest, the car starts to make a strange thumping sound. Aunt Lucy looks worried.

"I think we've got a puncture," she says. When they get out of the car, they can see that one of the front tires is flat.

"Come on," says Aunt Lucy. "We need to look in the trunk to find the spare tire, the blue tool box, and the instruction book, and we need to hurry!"

Can you find the things they need?

To change the tire, Aunt Lucy needs to loosen the four wheel nuts. She knows the end of the wrench must be the same shape as the wheel nuts.

Do you know which wrench she should use?

Then Aunt Lucy uses a jack to lift the car off the ground.

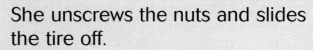

She unscrews the nuts and slides the tire off.

Then she puts on the spare tire and lowers the car to the ground.

Finally, she uses the wrench to tighten the wheel nuts.

Turning Town

As soon as Aunt Lucy has tightened the wheel nuts, they race to Turning Town. In the town, the one-way streets are narrow and winding. Dan tries to follow the route on the map, but they soon become lost.

"I'm sorry Aunt Lucy, but we'll have to stop for a few minutes while I figure out where we are," says Dan.

"No problem," replies Aunt Lucy. "We can both have a look at the map."

Do you know where they are on the map?

One way

Map of Turning Town

To Six Bridges

"Now we know where we are, we need to head toward Six Bridges, to rejoin the rally," says Dan.

Which way should they go to rejoin the rally?

Broken bridges

They soon reach Six Bridges, at the edge of Turning Town. On the other side of the river, several rally cars are zooming into the distance.

Aunt Lucy is about to drive over the widest bridge, when Dan suddenly stops her.

"Wait!" he says. "I don't think this bridge is safe. We'll have to choose another."

Can you see which bridge is safe to cross?

"If we don't cross here, we'll have to go the long way around," says Dan. "It's 30 miles, so even if we drive at 60 miles an hour, it will add lots of time to our journey."

How long would it take them to go the long way around if they drove at 60 miles per hour?

More fuel

Dan and Aunt Lucy drive carefully over the safe bridge. As they reach the other side, a red light starts flashing on the dashboard.

"We need to stop at a service station," says Aunt Lucy. "We're running out of fuel."

Dan looks for a service station on his map.

"Take the next left turn," he says. "Then turn right, then right again, over the bridge and right at a cross roads."

Can you follow Dan's directions and find the way to the service station?

As they drive toward the service station, Dan and Aunt Lucy notice a clanking sound.

"I think something will need fixing when we get to the service station," says Aunt Lucy. "And I think I know what it is."

Can you see what needs to be fixed?

Overtaken

After they've filled the car with fuel and fixed the bumper, Dan and Aunt Lucy drive on toward the finish line.

As they speed through Gearshift Gully, the road turns into a bumpy, dusty track. Aunt Lucy looks at the signs by the side of the track and quickly slows down.

What do you think the signs mean?

Just then, the Fume Brothers zoom past, stirring up thick clouds of dust.

"They're driving too fast," says Aunt Lucy, as she struggles to see the track.

When the dust clears, Dan notices the brothers have left a trail of trouble.

Can you spot the differences?

Crash!

Dan and Aunt Lucy continue on their way, but they don't get very far. Just around the corner, the Fume Brothers have crashed into a tree. A small crowd has gathered around them.

"What happened here?" asks Dan.

Everybody begins to talk at once. Dan listens carefully to everyone and tries to put their stories into the right order.

Can you put the stories into the right order and figure out what happened?

Can you see why the blue rally car had stopped?

Helping an old friend

A few miles down the road, Dan spots another broken down-rally car. As they drive nearer, Aunt Lucy recognizes her old driving instructor, Mr. Indicator. They slow down to ask him if he needs help.

"My car's engine needs more oil," he says. "But the other two bottles of oil that were strapped to the roof have rolled off. Can you help me find them?"

Can you see the lost bottles of oil?

"My old car is wonderful," says Mr. Indicator. "But if I drive over 30 miles per hour, it breaks down. It'll take me ages to reach the finish line."

If he sticks to 30 miles an hour, how long will it take Mr. Indicator to drive the last 90 miles to the finish line?

Nearly there

As they wave goodbye to Mr. Indicator, Aunt Lucy turns on the turbo-booster. The engine starts to roar as they zoom along the road. Soon they reach the last town before the finish line.

"We need to find a quick route through the town," says Dan. "Avoiding any road works or traffic lights, because they could slow us down."

Can you see which route they should take?

Dan leans over to see the dashboard and check their speed. But he can't remember which instrument to look at.

Can you remember which instrument shows speed?

Great Car Rally

To the finish →

At the finish line

The crowd starts to cheer as Aunt Lucy and Dan race around the final corner.

In a flash, they cross the finish line. Dan quickly figures out their rally time. They started at eight-thirty that morning and finished at seven-thirty in the evening.

Can you figure out how long the rally has taken them?

Dan and Aunt Lucy wait for the other rally cars to finish. Whose time is the fastest? When the judge announces the winners, Aunt Lucy and Dan realize they have won the Great Car Rally!

Wilma Wheelspin and Angus Automatic didn't finish the rally. Do you know why? (You'll have to look back through the book to find out what happened to them.)

A week later

The following weekend, Dan helps Aunt Lucy to check the car's engine. Then he lays out the Great Car Rally maps.

"We drove 200 miles in the morning, plus 50 miles to Turning Town," says Dan. "In the afternoon, we picked up speed and drove 350 miles."

How many miles did they drive in all?

As Dan and Aunt Lucy remember the adventures they had, a car pulls into the workshop. It looks very different than the last time Dan saw it.

Can you figure out who the car belongs to?

Answers

Pages 4–5 At the starting line

The cars are circled.

Dan and Aunt Lucy started the rally at 8:30am.

Pages 6–7 Which way?

The road to Axle Mountain is circled.

A yellow flashing light means the oil level is low.

Pages 8–9 Trouble ahead

The dangers are circled.

Aunt Lucy has changed to first gear (page 3).

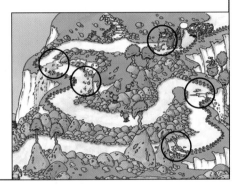

Pages 10–11 Forest trails

The route out of the forest is marked.

They have been traveling for three hours.

Pages 12–13 Puncture problem

The things they need are circled.

Aunt Lucy should use the right-hand wrench.

Pages 14–15 Turning Town

The circle marks where they are.

The route they should take is marked.

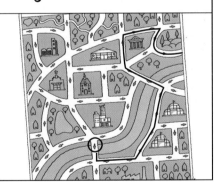

Pages 16–17 Broken bridges

The safe bridge is circled.

It would take them half an hour to drive the long way around.

Pages 18–19 More fuel

The route to the service station is marked.

The front bumper needs to be fixed.

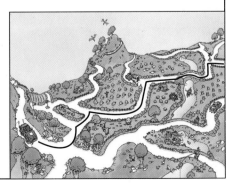

Answers

Pages 20–21 Overtaken

The signs mean "falling rocks" and "bends in the road".

The differences are circled.

Pages 22–23 Crash!

The stories are numbered.

The blue rally car stopped because it had two punctured tires.

Pages 24–25 Helping an old friend

The bottles of oil are circled.

It will take Mr. Indicator 3 hours to drive to the finish line.

Pages 26–27 Nearly there

The route they should take is marked.

The speedometer shows speed.

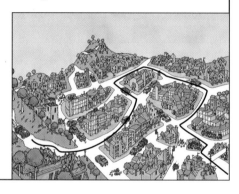

Pages 28–29 At the finish line

The rally had taken them 11 hours.

Wilma Wheelspin crashed into the river (page 19).

Angus Automatic was attacked by bears (page 11).

Page 30 A week later

They drove 600 miles in all.

The car belongs to Mr. Indicator (page 25).

Film Crew

Did you remember to look out for a member of the film crew on each double page?

First published in 2000 by Usborne Publishing Limited, Usborne House, 83-85 Saffron Hill, London EC1N 8RT, England.
www.usborne.com © Copyright 1999 Usborne Publishing Ltd. The name Usborne and the device ⊕ are Trade Marks of Usborne Publishing Ltd.